THIS BLOOMSBURY BOOK

BELONGS TO

....

*For Stuart who showed me the colours, and
Stuart J, Graeme and Cara, who keep them
bright - LS*

*To Joe
Lots of love from Great Uncle David! - DW*

First published in Great Britain in 2003 by Bloomsbury Publishing Plc
38 Soho Square, London, W1D 3HB

This paperback edition first published in 2004

A CIP catalogue record of this book is available from the British Library

ISBN 0 7475 6355 1

Printed in China

3 5 7 9 10 8 6 4 2

All papers used by Bloomsbury Publishing are natural, recyclable
products made from wood grown in well-managed forests. The
manufacturing processes conform to the environmental regulations of the
country of origin.

What Colour is Love?

BLOOMSBURY
CHILDREN'S
BOOKS

by Linda Strachan
illustrated by David Wojtowycz

"What colour is love?"
asked Small Smooth and Grey.

"Could it be green?"

Said old wrinkly Grandad,

"I don't know if that's true,

but grass is green –
so love might be blue."

"What colour is love?"

asked Small Smooth and Grey.
"Could it be blue?"

Tiger turned over
and rolled on his back.

"I can't tell you the answer,
my little fellow,

the sky is blue –
maybe love could be yellow?"

"What colour is love?"
asked Small Smooth and Grey.

"Could it be yellow?"

Lion opened an eye, too tired to play.

He yawned and he said,
"This hot sun is yellow –
isn't love red?"

"What colour is love?"
asked Small Smooth and Grey.
"Could it be red?"

Parrot looked down
from his perch in the tree.

"Red is for flowers, but love is so bright,
it's really quite simple – love must be white!"

"What
colour
is love?"

asked
Small Smooth and Grey.

"Could it be white?"

"No,
love isn't
white,"

said Zebra.

"No, I think ...
love is so wonderful –

it must be pink!"

"What colour is love?"

asked Small Smooth and Grey.

"Could it be pink?"

"Pink?"

screeched Flamingo.

"No, that can't be right.
Love should be orange
like the sunset at night."

Tired and exhausted
at the end of the day,
"I know who to ask,"
said Small Smooth and Grey.

He left Flamingo
     with his tall slender legs,

and passed by Zebra
          on the old river bed.

Lion had gone from his rock in the sun,

and Tiger, out hunting,

set off at a run.

He went to the water and dipped in his toe.
He said to his mother, "Does nobody know?
I've tried all the colours, from the grass to the flowers,
from the sky, to the clouds,
to the sun up above ...

but no one could tell me
the colour of
love."

"What colour is love?
I'll tell you little one ...

It's as dark
as the night

and as bright
as the sun.

Imagine a colour
and love is right there,

love is every colour,
everything,
everywhere.

"What colour is love?
Every colour,

all around …
… because nothing
else matters

when it's Love that
you've found."

Enjoy more great picture books from Bloomsbury Children's Books ...

Goodnight Lulu
Paulette Bogan

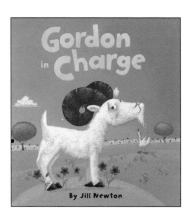

Gordon in Charge
Jill Newton

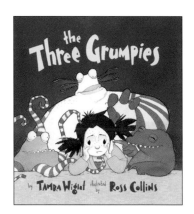

The Three Grumpies
Tamra Wight & Ross Collins

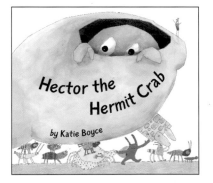

Hector the Hermit Crab
Katie Boyce

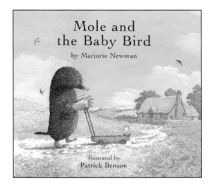

Mole and the Baby Bird
Marjorie Newman & Patrick Benson